I0726549

The Adventurous Princess

and other feminist fairy tales

written and illustrated by

Erin-Claire Barrow

Copyright © Erin-Claire Barrow 2019

All rights reserved. No part of this book may be reproduced or transmitted
by any person or entity, including internet search engines or retailers, in any
form or by any means, electronic or mechanical, including photocopying
(except under the statutory exceptions provisions of the *Australian Copyright
Act* 1968), recording, scanning or by any information storage and retrieval
system without the prior written permission of the publisher.

Published in 2019 by Publisher Obscura
an imprint of Odyssey Books

www.publisherobscura.com
www.odysseybooks.com.au

ISBN 978-1-925652-99-4 (hardcover)
ISBN 978-1-925652-72-7 (paperback)

Author's Foreword

I have always loved traditional fairy tales. They offer us the magic of bravely won happily-ever-after endings, true and enduring love, and worlds of enchantment and adventure. But these well-loved stories often reinforce rigid gender roles and norms, perpetuate stereotypes, and lack diversity in their characters.

Fairy tales that reward girls who are passive, obedient, or silent can reinforce the idea that girls shouldn't stand up for themselves and determine their own futures, instead relying on their beauty and kindness to ensure someone else takes care of them. Fairy tales that reward men who are handsome, brave, or clever with a princess to marry can reinforce the idea that women are prizes to be won. They often set unrealistic expectations for men to be competitive and aggressive, to be someone else's hero or saviour, and not to feel fear or anxiety.

In addition, fairy tales often lack diversity in their characters. The heroes and heroines of these traditional stories are usually either expressly or implicitly straight, white, young, able-bodied, and conventionally beautiful. It can be difficult for people in our diverse, modern society to see themselves represented in well-known and well-loved stories. This lack of diversity shapes what is valued in society and who we expect to see as the heroes of our stories.

In *The Adventurous Princess and other feminist fairy tales*, I have retold and illustrated nine traditional fairy tales with a feminist twist. I began retelling these stories because I wanted to read and share fairy tales that had the charm of the traditional stories but were more relatable for a modern audience.

I chose fairy tales to retell that are mostly well-known but contain elements that have always made me uncomfortable. From a princess who is defined purely by her delicacy in *The Princess and the Pea* to a kidnapped bride in *The Swan Maiden*, these are stories that were in need of a strong, fierce reimagining of the heroine, or closer exploration of the expectations placed on the hero.

I feel we deserve better representation of our diverse society in the fairy tales we all know and love, fairy tales that challenge rather than embed stereotypes, and stories that inspire young people, and young women in particular, to see *themselves* as the strong, clever, and adventurous heroes of their own stories.

I hope you enjoy the fairy tales in *The Adventurous Princess* as much as I have enjoyed retelling and illustrating them.

The Princess and the Pea

Once upon a time, there lived a Prince who dreamed of adventure and loved nothing more than stories. In a castle that teetered on a cliff above a stormy ocean, the Prince would play his lute while imagining the lands beyond the sea and the strange creatures that might live there.

Alas for the Prince, the King and Queen were determined that he should spend his time in the princely pursuits of warfare, statecraft, and taxation. In their view, adventures were only worthwhile if undertaken in pursuit of power—and never for a story.

"My darling," said the Queen, "did you hear that Prince Oliver succeeded in slaying the dragon that was besieging his castle?"

"That would make a wonderful painting," mused the Prince.

"Son, how would you fancy meeting Prince Hugo, who recently returned from rescuing the golden princess from her tower?" the King asked eagerly.

"I'd rather write a story about it," said the Prince.

The King and Queen sighed. In their minds there were certain things a prince must do, and writing stories, playing music, and daydreaming were simply not among them.

One of the most important things a prince must do, the King and Queen were certain, was marry a true princess. Traditionally, a true princess might be found in a tower guarded by a dragon, or have brothers who had been enchanted by a wicked sorcerer. Unfortunately for the King and Queen, very few of these obvious princesses remained, so they had devised their own test for discovering if a girl was a true princess.

One night, a loud storm raged around the castle. Rain pelted the roof and cascaded down the walls, lightning created jagged shadows on the steps outside, and thunder rattled the panes in the windows. As the family were sitting at dinner there came a loud knock on the front door. The King was jolted out of a reverie about roast swan. The Queen stopped thinking about her favourite hunting horse. And the Prince, who had been reading a book under the table, quickly pretended he was busy eating dinner.

"Who could possibly be about in this weather?" exclaimed the King.

As they all looked toward the door, the butler appeared. Behind him stood a particularly bedraggled girl in long boots, riding clothes, and a soaking wet cloak. By her side stood a large boarhound, both of them dripping a puddle onto the stone floor.

"Your majesties," the butler began, "this young woman—"

"Princess," interrupted the girl.

"Ahem, yes, this Princess was knocking at the door. She is looking for shelter from the storm."

The King and Queen exchanged a swift glance. This certainly sounded promising, even if the girl was dressed a little oddly for a princess.

"Do come in, my dear," the Queen said kindly.

"Please warm yourself by the fire," the King offered with concern.

"What were you doing out in the storm?" the Prince wondered aloud.

Once the Princess was warm and dressed in what the Queen considered to be much more suitable garments, they returned to dinner. The Princess ate as though she hadn't seen food for a month.

"You seem very hungry, my dear," remarked the Queen.

"I haven't had a decent meal for days," the Princess said between mouthfuls. "It's been a terrible week for adventuring. I got lost in a forest, chased by a dragon, and then caught in this storm."

"Adventuring?" said the Queen, with a concerned glance at her son, whose whole attention was fixed on the Princess, his fork halfway to his mouth.

After dinner, the Queen said she had *just* the room for a Princess. The Prince sighed, knowing all too well what his parents had in mind. He reluctantly showed the Princess to her room and she marched inside, only to stop halfway in, hands on hips, to contemplate the bed.

And what a bed it was! Twenty
mattresses were piled one on top of
the other and on top of those lay
twenty eiderdown quilts. A lad-
der reached all the way to the
top so the poor Princess could
get into the bed.

"Oh dear," said the Prince,
blushing quite red. "The
princess test."

The Princess gave him a
bemused look and with some
effort the Prince lifted the
bottom mattress to show her a
dried pea placed in the middle of
the bed.

He reluctantly explained that his
parents believed the pea would cause so
much discomfort to a true princess, who by
her very nature would be incredibly delicate, that
she would not be able to sleep all night.

The Princess stared and then started laughing. "Delicate!" she gasped when she caught
her breath. "Tell that to the bandits I fought last week! Or the dragon! I must remember
this next time I'm sleeping on a lumpy forest floor somewhere while off adventuring."

Sheepishly, the Prince joined in the laughter. "I was hoping if you weren't too tired
you might tell me about your adventures," he asked.

"Right," said the Princess. "Help me get a mattress down so we have somewhere sensible to sit."

The Princess told stories until the morning light crept through the window and
around the pile of mattresses on the bed. The Prince listened raptly to tales of fearless
exploration, perilous enchantments, and narrow escapes. He told the Princess how he'd
like to write these adventures into a book of stories, but the Princess was adamant that
the best way to enjoy adventures was to have your own.

"Oh no, I couldn't," lamented the Prince. "I have to stay here and practise all manner
of dull and princely things."

"I have an idea," said the Princess, a determined look in her eye.

That morning the Queen asked the Princess how she had slept.

"I didn't sleep a wink all night," replied the Princess, which was quite true.

The Queen was immensely happy and quickly called for the King. Finally, it seemed they had found a true princess. With a great sense of ceremony they declared that she was indeed a princess and welcomed her to stay in the castle and wed the Prince.

"Thank you kindly," said the Princess, holding in a bubble of laughter. "But my family has very strict ideas about princes—almost as strict as your ideas about princesses—and the Prince simply hasn't had enough adventures yet to keep them happy."

She looked around as the Prince came running toward them, carrying a bag overflowing with books, quills, inks, and paper, with his lute thrown over his shoulder.

"Do you mean he hasn't fulfilled enough quests?" asked the King.

"He hasn't slain very many dragons, it's true," admitted the Queen.

"Adventures for the sake of adventure," the Princess said boldly. "Adventures for the sake of stories, full of music and art and imagination!" She pulled the Prince up behind her onto her horse. With a flourish of her hat and a wave to the rather shocked King and Queen standing by the castle door, the Princess wheeled her horse and she and the Prince galloped toward the harbour.

Cinderella

Once upon a time, there lived an old woman named Ella. Among her neighbours, Ella was known for being kind, for being able to solve any problem, and for being able to talk to birds. Ella's only fault, they would say, was that she was perhaps too kind to her only son, who had grown into an arrogant and selfish man.

A time came when Ella's son decided to marry, and he brought his new bride and her two daughters to live with him in Ella's house. Ella soon found that her son and his wife were well matched in temperament and although the two girls meant well, they often left tasks half-finished and expected Ella to clean up after them.

Ella encouraged the girls to take an interest in the things that brought her joy, such as books, songs, and hard work in the fresh air. They would only sit by the window and sigh, however, waiting for life to find them, or gaze into a mirror, perfecting every detail of hair and dress in case the moment should come when their beauty would determine their future.

Soon Ella found herself working from dawn to dusk to keep the house and provide for the whims of her relatives. Her patience was sorely tested, but in her kindness she continued to hope, contrary to all reason, that her family would come to appreciate her hard work and care for her as she cared for them.

Although Ella was good at solving problems, she could not solve her own. And although Ella could speak to the birds and tell them her troubles, birds do not understand human troubles and they could not help her either. Eventually Ella was to be found most days in drudgery and often slept exhausted by the kitchen fire. When she served the family their meals, they would comment on the soot and cinders on her ragged dress and call her Cinderella.

The city Ella lived in was ruled by an old King. It was well known that the King was worried that his only child, a son, was easily distracted and lacked the good judgment to rule wisely. With no Queen and no words of wisdom to be had from his advisers, the King was at quite a loss as to what to do.

Ella's kind heart did not like to hear the gossip spreading in the city. She wrote three words on a tiny piece of paper and bade one of her birds drop it by the King's feet. The

King was pacing anxiously in the royal garden when a cautious finch dropped the paper before him. On it he found written:

Hold a ball.

Unfortunately, the King did not have Ella's powers of deduction and did not understand the hint. Ella sent another message. This time, the King was hurrying past the royal stables when a cheeky robin dropped a scrap of paper on his head that said:

Invite all the women in the kingdom.

The King put two and two together and thought it sounded a rather lovely idea, but it didn't stop him worrying about the Prince. Ella, continuing to hear the gossip in the city, sent a third message. The King was hastening through the royal courtyard when a bold wren dropped a note that read:

Hope a sensible one chooses to marry him.

"Ah ha!" cried the King, and immediately sent for his heralds to announce three days of royal festivities, crowned by a ball at which the Prince would choose his bride—or she would choose him.

On the evening of the ball, Ella looked in her cupboards and shelves for a suitable dress and found every last one had been sold off or snipped up to provide for her family. While she tapped her foot and began to think of a solution, her daughter-in-law came by and saw Ella's intentions.

"Why Cinderella, surely you are not planning to go to the ball! You are too old to enjoy it, and just think of your poor granddaughters returning home hungry and cold if you are not here to keep the fire lit and make supper for them."

Ella sighed and began her usual tasks and chores, but as she heard her family leaving in the carriage, she suddenly felt a spark of fire she hadn't felt for many months.

"I *will* go to the ball," said Ella determinedly, "even if I go in rags!"

No sooner had she spoken than she heard a whoosh and a flutter and turned to find a small, gnarled old woman, much older than Ella herself, sitting by the fireplace where no one had been a moment before.

"Well, well, well," said the old woman. "Not my usual line of work I must admit. You look like you almost had a solution figured out."

"Almost," replied Ella, somewhat bewildered. "But you are…?"

"Here to make it all a bit more straightforward!" cried the old woman, leaping up with a nimbleness that quite belied her age and pulling out of her shawl a twig that she tapped three times against her hand. With another whoosh and a flutter Ella found herself outside, standing by a stylish open carriage drawn by two white horses. Ella looked down and saw that her rags had turned into a shimmery dress made of yards and yards of silk and gauze, under which she teetered in two little glass slippers.

"Fairy Godmother," Ella said tartly, having discovered the identity of the old woman, "I would not call this outfit 'straightforward'."

The old woman eyed Ella. "Usually they just wear what they're given," she said grumpily.

Ella suddenly found herself feeling unexpectedly bold. "Usually, I imagine, they're less than half my age and don't know how to stand up to you!"

"Oh very well then," said the old woman, and tapped the twig against her hand again. At once Ella found herself in a very smart and comfortable outfit, with a beautifully embroidered cloak and elegant boots with only a hint of glass in the buttons up the sides.

At the ball no one recognised Ella. The old King himself was very taken with the elegant lady who entered the hall, and he and Ella danced much of the night. The King greatly admired Ella's wisdom, kindness, and quick wit. He told Ella that the ball had only come about because of some mysterious messages passed on by birds.

"Fancy that," murmured Ella.

The King confided in Ella that he already had in mind several girls who he thought would make sensible queens and he hoped one would fancy the Prince.

"The only trouble," Ella said, glancing around, "is that love is even less straightforward than fairy godmothers…" And sure enough, there was the Prince, dancing with one of Ella's granddaughters, both with eyes only for each other.

"I suspect," said the King, "that I am going to need someone wise, patient, and kind if we are to make these two fit to rule. And there is no one I'd rather have at my side to do it. Have you ever fancied living in a palace?"

Ella only needed to think for a moment. She had made the decision to come to the ball and after all this time she was ready to make the decision to leave her family and their poor treatment of her.

"There's nothing I'd like better," Ella replied firmly. Suddenly a thought occurred to her. "To be quite honest though, I expect these fine clothes are going to turn into rags on the stroke of midnight and I'll have to run out of here before they do!"

"I'd run after you if need be," said the King, "but if there's one thing we have plenty of in a palace, it's fine clothes. Please do stay!"

The Swan Maiden

Long ago, a hunter lived on the shores of a wide lake. One evening, he saw seven swans alight on the banks of the lake and, shaking off their feathery robes, become the most enchanting women he had ever seen. As the swan maidens bathed in the lake, the hunter crept forward and stole the feathered robe of the youngest, hiding with it in the bushes.

When the swan maidens returned from the water they searched and searched for the stolen robe, but as dawn approached all except the youngest transformed back into swans and were forced to leave their sister behind.

After they had gone, the hunter approached the swan maiden with her robe in his hands. She cried and begged that he return her robe, but he would not, fearing she would fly away. He told the swan maiden that he loved her and that in the morning they would be married, then he took her back to his house on the lake's edge and hid her robe where she could not find it.

Now, perhaps when you think of a swan maiden, you imagine her elegance, her slender beauty, her delicate nature. Certainly, that is what the hunter imagined, as he planned their hasty wedding ceremony. But it may be that you have forgotten that swans are fierce and wild, strong from flying against the wind, and brave in the face of danger.

The swan maiden waited until the hunter had eaten his food and drunk his drink and was tired. Then with all the fierceness of a trapped creature, she flung him down and bound him to the foot of the bed.

"Where is it?" she hissed at him. But he would not tell her.

"Very well. I shall find it myself, but I shall show the same respect for your possessions as you have shown for mine." She tore apart the house, and each item she searched, she took out of the house and threw into the lake. Soon a large pile of the hunter's furniture and belongings were sinking into the shallow mud, for the swan maiden was both angry and strong.

Finally, in a small box in a dark corner of the last room, the swan maiden found her robe. With a cry of delight, she spun it about her shoulders. She leaped into the air, instantly transforming into a swan, and flew away without a backward glance at the huntsman or his empty house. And if someone has not freed him, he is likely there still.

Beauty and the Beast

Long ago in the midst of a dark forest there stood a forbidding castle, and in the castle lived a beast who was terrifying in both temper and appearance. She had not always been a beast; once she had been a beautiful and powerful princess, but her arrogance and selfishness had caused a sorceress to transform her so that her temper might be matched only by her appearance. This way she would stay until she learned to love and someone loved her in return.

The Beast lived alone in the castle for many years. Although the enchantment ensured her needs were met, it cared nothing for her loneliness and she saw naught of other living beings, for all avoided the fearsome creature. Over time the Beast grew somewhat kinder, as she tried to tempt birds and animals back into her garden, and less arrogant, as she had lost the beauty and power she earlier prized. Time moved on and people forgot the Beast, until those living by the edge of the dark forest might go their whole lives never once being warned of her.

One day, as a wild storm raged above the woods, a man entered the castle grounds, to the astonishment of the Beast watching furtively from the shadows. Wary of human company after so many years, the Beast stayed hidden but caused the castle to provide a feast and warm bed for the man. The next morning she watched him leave and was about to turn away when he reached up and broke a rose from the most beautiful rose tree in her garden.

The Beast sprung forward in a rage. "How dare you!" she growled in a terrifying voice. "I gave you shelter from the storm, provided you with good food and a safe place to stay, and this is how you repay me?" The Beast knocked the rose from his hand.

"Have mercy!" cried the man. "I meant no wrong! I am a poor merchant with nothing to my name and I hoped only to bring home a gift for my daughters."

The Beast demanded the merchant tell his full story, and as he talked she realised how much she had longed for human company. When he spoke about his daughters the Beast remembered the terms of the enchantment the sorceress had set. "Only when you love someone, and they love you in return, despite your terrifying appearance, will you regain your true form," she had said.

"I will forgive you and let you go," the Beast told the merchant, "and moreover I will send you home with riches such as will let you and your family live in comfort all your lives. But in return, you must send one daughter to stay and keep me company in this castle. I promise she will come to no harm and will want for nothing."

Although the merchant promised the Beast he would do so, the Beast could see in his eyes that he would say anything to escape her and expected little to come from his promise. She watched sadly as he went on his way.

Yet hardly a week had passed when a tall young woman with curious eyes and a confident smile rode self-assuredly up to the doors of the castle. The Beast again watched in secret as the young woman entered the castle and with growing confidence began to explore its many rooms and corridors. At last as night fell, the Beast caused a great banquet to be set in the main dining hall of the castle. The Beast entered the room shyly, trying to appear as small and unthreatening as possible for a creature of great height and terrifying appearance.

The young woman was startled and looked a little afraid, but she squared her shoulders and stepped bravely forward to meet the Beast. "My name is Beauty," she said. "Thank you for welcoming me to your castle."

"Odd name," said the Beast. "I mean, my apologies, my name is… er, Beast." She felt a little lost for words and was uncharacteristically worried that she might say something that would antagonise or upset this odd young woman. "I'm glad you're here," she finished awkwardly.

"Well," said Beauty, "so am I as it happens. I am always looking for a new adventure and this certainly sounded like one. I also always take people at their word and I was told I have yours that no harm will come to me here."

"Yes, yes, precisely," replied the Beast. "Everything you could wish for is yours here, just say the word."

"I also feel that my family owes you a debt," Beauty said solemnly. "Although it is not the custom in our part of the world to eat someone for stealing a rose, I understand stealing roses is a grave transgression here."

Was that a joke? the Beast wondered. Beauty raised an eyebrow before sitting herself down determinedly in front of the banquet laid out before them.

Each day Beauty was in the castle, the Beast endeavoured to find new things to distract and delight her, from the great castle library, to rooms of paintings and sculptures, to gardens in which roses were but the least of the charms. Beauty's boldness, ready humour, and calm nature charmed the Beast, and on the increasingly rare occasion the Beast let her arrogance or temper get the better of her, Beauty would never hesitate to hold her to account.

The Beast found she was looking at everyday occurrences in new ways. Each day was an adventure with Beauty, and what had once seemed mundane was now exciting and different. Small things like the sound of Beauty's voice as she laughed or sang in the

garden, the click of her cane echoing in the castle halls or her look of concentration as she tried something new made the Beast wake each morning joyful at spending time with her. As the days passed, the Beast became much less fearsome in temper, if not appearance.

As the Beast came to know and care for Beauty, she realised that this strange feeling, so new to her, was love. But she had no experience of being loved in return. Adored, perhaps. Feared, certainly. But not loved. How would she know if Beauty loved her? And besides, she thought, why would someone like Beauty ever love a Beast like her?

Beauty clearly enjoyed spending time with the Beast and in the castle and grounds, but one day the Beast noticed she seemed quiet and less interested in their usual adventures. When the Beast asked what ailed her, Beauty said that she missed her family terribly and wished she could see them. The Beast could not bear to see Beauty hurting and although she knew it might deny her all chance of undoing the enchantment, she released Beauty from her promise so that she might return home.

"Only please, please come back to me," begged the Beast. "My heart is heavy at the thought of being without you and if you are gone too long I do not know that I will survive."

Beauty assured the Beast she would return, but her gaze was torn between the Beast and the forest path that would take her home, and she was quickly away.

For weeks the Beast pined for Beauty and could barely eat nor sleep. When Beauty still did not return, the Beast felt her heart was breaking and she collapsed in sorrow under her rose trees. Barely conscious, she hardly heard as Beauty clattered into the castle grounds, calling for her, fear filling her voice when the Beast did not answer.

At last, Beauty found the Beast. She held her tight, sobbing as she struggled to wake her. "Oh Beast, I did not know how much you meant to me until you were no longer there. Please wake up. I love you and I cannot bear to be apart from you."

The Beast felt herself lifted up in that moment as though by strong hands. She caught a glimpse of Beauty's shocked face as the sound of a thousand bells rang out at once and light flared through the garden. The Beast felt herself placed on her feet and she held her hands out in front of her wonderingly, for they were human hands, and when she looked down she found herself once again in her human form.

Beauty looked at strange lady before her, bewildered.

"But, where is my Beast?" she cried.

"Right here," replied the lady, touching Beauty lightly on the arm. "It was always me, under an enchantment, and now I am free to tell you the whole story. But first, you had best call me Angeline."

The Frog Prince

O nce upon a time there was a Prince, who lived in a pond in the gardens of a castle. Perhaps you are wondering why a Prince would live in a pond. Well, this Prince had found himself on the wrong end of an enchantment, which had turned him into a frog the colour and size of a smooth river pebble—mottled brown and just big enough to fit snugly in the palm of your hand.

The poor frog Prince was deeply unhappy. The only way to break the enchantment was for him to find a princess willing to give him her companionship and let him sit next to her, eat from her plate, and sleep in her bed. And how was a frog to catch the attention of a princess, much less have her choose to be his companion?

One day the frog was moping in the middle of the pond when he heard a sound. Looking up, he saw the youngest princess from the castle, weeping by the edge of the pond.

"Why are you crying, Princess?" he asked.

The Princess looked around and was startled to see the voice came from a small frog sitting on a lily pad. "Oh frog!" she exclaimed, "my golden ball has fallen into the pond and I cannot get it back, for the water is too deep."

The frog had a good heart, and was about to fetch her ball, when he had an idea.

"Princess," he called. "What will you give me in return for your ball?"

"Why anything, you funny little frog," said the young Princess. "Gold, jewels, whatever you wish."

"I don't want gold or jewels," said the frog, "but if you promise to be my companion, and let me sit by your side, eat from your plate, and sleep in your bed, I will fetch the ball."

The Princess looked at the frog, who lived in the pond, and looked up the hill to the castle where she lived. They were worlds apart. With a shrug, she gave her promise. The frog quickly brought up her ball, but no sooner did she have it than she skipped back to the castle, completely forgetting both the frog and her promise.

The frog took all day to follow her up to the castle on his short legs, arriving out of breath as the family were sitting down to supper. He knocked at the door and the youngest Princess opened it, then with a look of horror quickly closed it again, shutting the frog outside.

"Who is it?" the frog heard a man ask.

"Oh father, it is a frog!" cried the Princess. "He fetched my ball, which had fallen in the pond, and in return I promised to be his companion. I thought he could not leave the pond and could not possibly mean what he had asked."

"Open the door," said the King, and the Princess did so, letting the frog hop inside. The frog reminded the Princess of her promise. She was clearly uncomfortable at the idea of being his companion, but when the King heard what she had promised, he commanded that she put the frog by her on the table and feed him from her plate.

Eventually the frog grew tired, and asked that the Princess take him to her bed to sleep. The young Princess began to cry, for she did not want to sleep beside a cold, slimy frog. The King felt uneasy, but he told his daughter that promises were important and must not be broken.

At this, the Queen stood up. "Right, that is quite enough," she said crisply. With a stern look at the King, she turned to the youngest Princess. "My darling, you need never let anyone in your bed that you are not entirely comfortable with having there, regardless of anything you have said or done before." Turning to the frog, she said, "And as for you, that was an entirely inappropriate request of a young princess!"

The frog Prince was surprised. He hadn't thought that his request might upset the Princess. Considering it, he began to see that perhaps it was rather presumptuous. In fact, he realised that only he knew that if all went according to plan, the Princess would have woken up with a Prince in her bed instead of a frog, and he began to feel very awkward indeed.

The middle Princess noticed the frog was looking a little self-conscious. "Why do you want a princess for a friend anyway, Mr Frog? Why not a lizard, or a fish, or another frog?"

"Ah, well, you see… Oh, you'd never believe me," the frog said sadly.

"Try us," countered the oldest Princess.

"The thing is," said the frog, "I'm not really a frog." The family looked startled, but they weren't laughing, so he continued. "I'm actually a Prince, under a spell, and the only way to break the spell is to sit by the side of a Princess, eat from her plate, and sleep in her bed. Which is a rather forward thing to ask, I see now."

"A Prince? Truly!" said the oldest Princess with a chuckle. "Goodness me, that's easily settled. Leave my little sister alone and come up here by me." She picked up the frog and put him next to her. "Here, you may have some food from my plate," she said, feeding him a grape, "and after dinner you may spend the night on my pillow, but don't be getting ideas about hopping anywhere else!"

That night the frog slept, quiet and good as gold on the oldest Princess's pillow. He was woken with a bump and a thud in the morning, having suddenly become much too big for a pillow and fallen to the floor, as the enchantment unravelled and he regained his true form. The Prince leaped to his feet with a shout of joy, which immediately woke

the Princess, who looked at him in astonishment. He leaped about the room, jumping up to touch the ceiling, laughing and hugging the startled Princess.

All the noise brought the rest of the family, who stood in the doorway, speechless. The Prince hugged each of them, stopping in between to look at his own hands and feet in wonder.

Eventually the King gave the Prince a hearty pat on the back. "Well, well," he said. "Well, well, well."

A fine feast was held for the Prince and he was given new clothes and a horse with which to travel to his own land, for his own family were no doubt missing him greatly. The Princesses teased him about avoiding enchantments on the journey, and the Prince promised to write to them. Then he swung onto his horse, laughing with delight that he was now once again as tall as a horse, and galloped toward home.

Snow White

Once upon a time there lived a Queen, who was the most beautiful woman in the land. Now, you may say that it is impossible to objectively judge or compare beauty, or that true beauty is on the inside, but this Queen had a magic mirror that told her how beautiful she was, and the mirror's opinion was the only one she cared about.

Every morning the Queen would stand in front of the mirror and say, "Mirror mirror, on the wall, who is the fairest of them all?" And the mirror would reply, "You, oh Queen, are fairest of all."

The Queen had a step-daughter, called Snow White, of whom she was very fond. Snow White was usually an exuberant girl, full of energy and often to be found outside, falling in the mud chasing squirrels, or setting off on haphazard adventures to the edges of the royal garden. But lately, the Queen noticed that Snow White had become quiet and withdrawn. She picked at her food and hardly went outside the castle at all.

One morning, the Queen went to her mirror as usual, but from the doorway who did she see but Snow White, standing in front of the mirror as the Queen usually did, asking, "Mirror mirror, on the wall, who is the fairest of them all?" And to the Queen's horror, the mirror replied, "The Queen is very fair indeed, but not as fair as you will be."

The Queen was seized with a terrible jealousy. Look at her youth, she thought. Look at her perfect body—no wrinkles, no stretch marks. She clenched her hands into fists. Suddenly, she realised that Snow White was still talking to the mirror.

"What about this?" asked Snow White, pointing to her belly. "A bit chubby, but overall still beautiful," said the mirror. "What about these?" she asked, pointing to her freckles. "Maybe they'll go away as you get older," the mirror said dubiously. Snow White's lip started to tremble. The Queen, watching from the doorway, felt unexpectedly angry toward the mirror. Abruptly, she remembered when she had been a child, before she had the mirror and before anyone had started to tell her how beautiful she was. A tear rolled down her cheek as she thought of the little girl who scraped her knees climbing trees to peer into birds' nests, hair all tangled and face smudged with dirt.

The Queen looked at young Snow White, already beginning to worry about her looks and see her differences as flaws, and she saw the answer. In one motion, despite an inner voice that screamed at her not to, she lifted the mirror from the wall and threw it to the floor, where it broke into a thousand silent pieces.

She gathered Snow White into the biggest and warmest hug she could.

"You are perfect just the way you are," she said. "Especially those dear freckles!" Then the Queen took Snow White and they chased each other through the mud, ate an enormous breakfast, found all the birds' nests in the garden, and lived happily ever after.

Allerleirauh

Once upon a time, in a cold and bitter land, there ruled a King and Queen who had one child, a young daughter. The King was selfish, greedy, and cruel. He valued his kingdom for the wealth it could deliver him, not the people who lived in it, and he valued his wife for her extraordinary beauty and not for her kindness, wisdom, or courage.

One day the Queen grew ill and when she knew she would soon die she called the King to her. Hoping to spare her daughter from a stepmother who would not care for her, the Queen made the King promise he would not remarry unless to a woman as kind and wise as the Queen herself. The King swore he would do as she had asked.

Over time, as the King dwelled on his promise to the Queen and turned it over in his head, he felt that what he had really promised was to marry someone who was her equal.

"What was special about her was her beauty," he mused. "Someone her equal would be someone as beautiful to me as she was."

Unfortunately, when the Queen had set the conditions for remarriage, she had not counted on the need to spare her daughter from the King. The King demanded his advisers begin a search of the kingdom for a woman he would desire to marry, but as the search continued and the Princess grew up, it became evident that she was the very image of her mother. The King began to mutter to his advisers that if he were to fulfil the terms of his promise there was only one girl he could marry—the Princess.

Now the Princess had not only inherited her mother's looks, but also her determination, courage, and wisdom. She resolved that nothing should force her into this terrible marriage and requested that before she could be married the King must have three dresses made for her: one as gold as the sun, one as silver as the moon, and one that sparkled like the stars. In addition to these, she must have a cloak made from a piece of fur from each animal in the kingdom.

The Princess hoped that she had set an impossible condition—for who could create such clothes?—but if there was one thing she had learned, setting conditions was no assurance of safety. While the King ordered the clothes made, she used the time well and went to the King's advisers, to the ladies and lords of the kingdom, to the powerful men who commanded the armies, and those who oversaw the law. She bade each one ask the King to revoke his decision, or if he would not, to force him to step aside and let the Princess rule as Queen in her own right.

Each person avoided her gaze. Although horrified, they looked about and thought that their own wealth and station depended on the King's favour and they were afraid to cross him. Instead they provided excuses, suggesting a daughter should obey her father and a princess should not gainsay a king.

When the impossible dresses and cloak were presented to the Princess, she was not surprised and knew she must seek help from further afield. She folded each dress up so small it fit inside a walnut shell, then she put these shells in her pocket, threw on the cloak of many furs and crept out of the castle in the dead of night.

The Princess walked for several nights, hiding during the day, until she could be sure she had passed beyond the borders of her father's kingdom. One day as she slept inside a hollow tree she was woken by the sound of a hunting party. When the Princess emerged, the party did not know what to make of the ragged girl in the fur cloak. Wary of these strangers, the Princess told them she was a poor orphan and begged for work at the palace. They called her Allerleirauh, which meant 'all kinds of fur', and in the palace she was sent to the kitchen, where she carried wood and water, made the simplest of dishes, and swept the ashes from the fire.

Allerleirauh was not prepared to spend the rest of her life hiding herself. She planned to get her kingdom back and cast out her father, the wicked King. She worked hard in the kitchen, and she watched the people around her. She learned that they were not afraid of their Queen, that each person was of equal worth and that people went out of their way to help each other. To each servant Allerleirauh met, she told her story as if it had happened to someone else. At the end, she asked each one what they would do if they were the girl in her story. All told her they would take their case before the Queen, who was wise and bold.

One day it was announced that three nights of festivities would be held for the Prince's birthday. Allerleirauh begged leave of the cook to watch.

"You may go," said the cook, "only mind you stay outside the door so you do not shock the guests with your appearance, all sooty and covered in fur!"

Allerleirauh quickly went to her room and took off her cloak. Scrubbing the soot off her face and hands, she put on the dress as golden as the sun and went to the ball. There everyone stepped out of her way, for no one knew her, and in her golden dress they believed she must be royalty. The strange princess danced with the knights, baronets, and noble ladies. To each one she danced with, she told her story as if it had happened to a girl who worked in their kitchens, and asked their advice. Each one told her they would take their case before the Queen.

One the second day of festivities, Allerleirauh again asked the cook if she could watch through the door and the cook gave the same answer. Instead of watching, Allerleirauh washed the soot off her face and hands, put on the dress as silver as the moon, and went to the ball. Again, everyone at the ball wondered at the stranger in their midst. That

night she danced with dukes and duchesses, counts and countesses, and the Prince himself. Again, she told her story to all she danced with and received the same advice.

On the last night, Allerleirauh again asked the cook if she could watch the festivities. She washed the soot from her face and hands and put on her dress that sparkled like the stars, but over the top she threw the cloak of many furs. When she entered the ballroom all stood back, and each was reminded of the girl from the story the stranger had told. Allerleirauh approached the throne at the front of the room and asked to speak to the Queen. The Queen, curious, bade her tell her tale. Allerleirauh related all that had befallen her, sparing no detail. At the end she threw off the cloak and was revealed as the stranger from the past two nights of the ball, and she begged the Queen for her help.

"I see before me a woman who is brave, resourceful, and clever," mused the Queen. "An injustice has been done to you and I applaud your courage in overcoming it. Tell me, if you ruled your kingdom, what would you bring to it that your father does not?"

"I have seen the way people in your kingdom from the lowest to the highest are not afraid of their rulers and look to them for guidance rather than obeying them from desire for favour," said Allerleirauh. "I have seen that people in your kingdom care for everyone, not just the powerful, and are happy to help others where they can. If I ruled that is what I would bring to my kingdom."

"Well said," cried the Queen. "I believe you would." She called her ladies and lords to her side. "I am determined that we will see your land in your hands and bring down this man who has shown himself to be as unfit a king as he was a father. My finest advisers and I shall return with you to your kingdom and negotiate on your behalf, and together we shall see justice done."

Then the Queen and Allerleirauh journeyed forth to Allerleirauh's kingdom, and the wicked King was forced to depart. Allerleirauh ruled wisely and well. She often sought advice from her neighbour the Queen, and the two lands prospered.

The Goose Girl

There was once a young doctor who set out to make her fortune in the world. Her family sent her on her way with gifts that included jewels, books, and fine clothes, as well as a talking horse that they called Falada. Her mother wept tears of joy to see her daughter following her dreams and gave her a handkerchief with three drops of blood to carry her mother's protection wherever she went.

The young doctor hired three attendants to accompany her on her travels. The chief of these, the young doctor's assistant, was training to be a doctor herself. She was graceful and charming, enchanting everyone she met, but her charm hid jealousy and cunning ambition.

As the four travelled, the young doctor took the opportunity to practise her craft and learn from the wise women and men of the areas she passed through. The attendants scoffed and disparaged the local knowledge, preferring to spend their time in pubs and inns, drinking and carousing.

The further they went from home, the drier the land became and the warmer the days. Falada was strong and brave and carried the young doctor proudly, but the attendants' horses were older beasts that walked with heads drooping and hooves dragging in the sandy dirt.

One day they came across a cool, clear creek passing beside the dusty road. The young doctor turned to her assistant and asked her to please draw some water for the group.

The assistant looked at her shrewdly. "We'll each kneel by the creek and get our own water. You're no better than the rest of us."

This seemed fair to the young doctor, who knelt by the creek to drink from her little golden cup. At her breast, where she had put the handkerchief from her mother, she heard a small voice say, "If your mother only knew, her heart would surely break in two." It was a little melodramatic, the young doctor thought.

A little further on the group again grew thirsty. This time, when the young doctor asked her assistant to draw some water, the assistant demanded the young doctor fetch the water for the rest of the group. Hoping to appease her, the young doctor did so, and again she heard the small voice from her handkerchief cry, "If your mother only knew, her heart would surely break in two." Possibly true, thought the young doctor, frowning.

A third time the group stopped for water, and once more the assistant made the young doctor fetch the water. As she leaned down the handkerchief slipped free. It fluttered a

moment on the wind before being caught in the water and swiftly washed away. Behind the young doctor the assistant smiled as she watched the mother's protection disappear around a bend in the creek.

As the young doctor returned to the group, she saw that her assistant was now mounted on Falada and one of the older horses had been left for the young doctor.

"You will ride my nag now, and I will ride Falada," the assistant announced haughtily as her accomplices watched. "And when we arrive at the next town, *I* will be the doctor and you the assistant. Swear you will tell no one or we will leave you in this inhospitable land with nothing and you will surely die." The young doctor was forced to swear, through bitter tears, as the assistant took her books, jewels, and fine clothes. She had little doubt that with the assistant's charm and the support of the other two attendants few would believe her word against theirs.

They soon arrived at a town and the false doctor introduced herself to the Mayor, a stern, sharp woman with a heavy cane and slate-grey hair. The town did not have a doctor and the Mayor offered the false doctor a beautiful house if she would stay. The false doctor agreed, but pointing at the true doctor she said, "The heat of the desert has addled this one's wits and she is no use to me. Perhaps you could find her some work to keep her from idleness."

So the young doctor was sent to a farm on the edge of the town where she was put to work watching over a flock of geese. The farmer was a kind-hearted man. He noticed that the new goose girl was generous and caring toward all the animals, and particularly helpful when they were sick. He was puzzled that she had been described as dull and slow; to him she seemed fiercely intelligent, though often quiet and withdrawn.

Meanwhile the false doctor used the books, notes, and medicines she had stolen to convince the town of her credentials, and although there was some grumbling about the cures she produced, she managed well enough that the town had no reason to suspect her.

Each time she passed the stables, however, she saw the reproachful looks of Falada and was fearful that her secret would be shared. She asked the Mayor to kill the horse, saying it had proven on the journey to be quite useless and untameable. The Mayor had heard that the farmer's new goose girl worked well with animals and so, unbeknownst to the false doctor, she sent Falada to the farm.

Each morning, as the goose girl passed Falada she would say, "Alas Falada, standing there," and Falada would reply, "Alas young doctor, passing by. If your mother only knew, her heart would surely break in two."

One morning, the farmer saw this exchange and was greatly puzzled, but the goose girl would not be drawn to explain it. Curious, he told the story to the Mayor, who determined to see this strange occurrence for herself. She rose early and hid behind the barn, and as the goose girl went by she heard her say, "Alas Falada, waiting there." And Falada

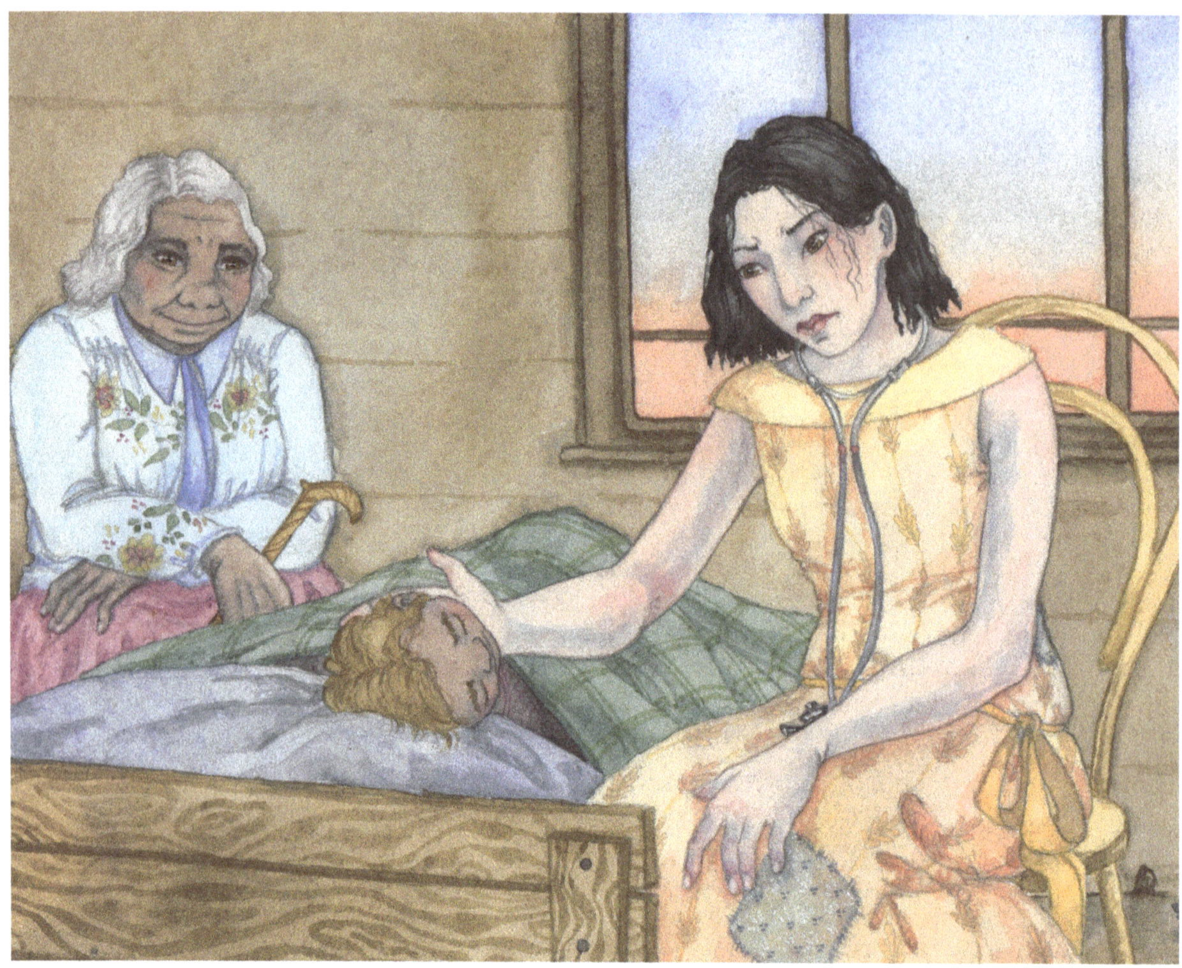

replied, "Alas young doctor, passing by. If your mother only knew, her heart would surely break in two."

Now, the Mayor was perceptive, and she remembered that the goose girl had arrived with the new doctor. She began to piece together a theory in her mind and to test it she invited the goose girl to visit her house.

"I have heard how clever you are with sick animals," the Mayor said. "I have a young'un at my place that is poorly. Perhaps you could come by and see if you can help?"

The goose girl went with the Mayor to her house, and when she arrived she found that rather than the sick animal she expected, it was the Mayor's own grandchild who was ill. The little boy tossed and turned, hot with fever, and the Mayor explained that the nature of the illness utterly eluded the town's new doctor, who had been unable to help. The goose girl was able without trouble to diagnose the mysterious illness and recommend a remedy, which quickly took effect. Soon the little boy was recovered and playing in the garden with his sisters once more.

The wise mayor guessed what had truly happened and she presented the story to the erstwhile goose girl, who cried in relief at finally being able to tell someone that she was indeed the true doctor.

That night a festival was held in the town and at dinner the Mayor sat at the head of the table with the false doctor on one side of her and the true doctor on the other. In the excitement of the festival, the false doctor did not recognise the true. As the night progressed, the Mayor turned to the false doctor and said she would ask her a riddle—what punishment was deserved by a person who stole a livelihood and put others' lives at risk by pretending to be someone they were not?

"Why, they should be thrown into the desert to die!" the false doctor declared obliviously.

"Humph, we are not so cold-hearted as you," said the Mayor, "but you shall be on your way this very night, with naught but what you came in with." And with that, the false doctor and the two attendants were cast out of the town and the young doctor welcomed. The town rejoiced and the young doctor joined in, glad that she could once again practise her craft and make her fortune in the world.

The Little Mermaid

Once there was a little mermaid, who lived in a great palace on the ocean floor. In her kingdom the fishes were her companions, her garden overflowed with colourful sea grasses that swayed in the currents, and her family loved her. But the little mermaid was unhappy. All her life she had dreamed of seeing the world above the ocean, and on her fifteenth birthday she had finally been allowed to visit. That very day, she had fallen in love with a handsome prince on board a ship and saved his life when a terrible storm broke the ship apart.

The little mermaid pined for the prince. She no longer found enjoyment in singing with her sisters, though her voice was the most lovely of all, or in swimming with the dolphins and fishes. All day and all night, she imagined going to the land and finding the Prince. She dreamed of hearing about his world, and telling him about hers.

Finally, when she could bear the longing no more, the little mermaid visited an old sea witch, who lived in the wild ocean forest near the palace.

"I know what you want," said the sea witch as she approached. "You want to be with your prince."

"Oh yes," replied the little mermaid.

"You want to give up your beautiful tail for two legs, and walk on the land as he does."

"I suppose, yes," said the little mermaid.

"Very well," said the sea witch. "But magic is not without its price. When your tail turns into legs you will feel great pain, and every step you take on your new feet will be agony, as though standing on sharp knives."

"I… I can do it," trembled the little mermaid.

"You will never be able to return to the ocean," said the sea witch. "Never see your family again."

The little mermaid was silent.

"And what's more," said the sea witch, "you must give up your beautiful voice in order for the spell to work."

"My voice!" cried the little mermaid. "But how shall I talk to him? How shall I get to know him and he get to know me?"

"Not my problem," said the sea witch. "You've got expressive eyes, use them. Likely he'll tell you all about himself, and do you really care if he doesn't know anything about you?"

"Well, yes," said the little mermaid. "Actually I do! And actually, I like talking!" The little mermaid looked down at her tail. "And actually, I like my tail!" And with a big swoosh she was off, out of the sea witch's house as fast as she could swim.

The sea witch laughed and dusted her hands together. "That's my good deed for the day," she said to the little fishes that swam around her. "Change her whole self to try to make someone love her. Well, I never." And with a quiet chuckle she went back to tending her garden.

www.ingramcontent.com/pod-product-compliance
Lightning Source LLC
Chambersburg PA
CBHW042044160726
48295CB00016B/958